Helpers in Our Community

MECHANICS

CHRISTINE HONDERS

New York

Published in 2020 by The Rosen Publishing Group, Inc.
29 East 21st Street, New York, NY 10010

Copyright © 2020 by The Rosen Publishing Group, Inc.

All rights reserved. No part of this book may be reproduced in any form without permission in writing from the publisher, except by a reviewer.

First Edition

Editor: Greg Roza
Book Design: Reann Nye

Photo Credits: Cover, p.1 Lopolo/Shutterstock.com; pp. 4–22 Abstractor/Shutterstock.com; p. 5 Studio 72/Shutterstock.com; p. 7 goodluz/Shutterstock.com; p. 9 Christina Richards/Shutterstock.com; p. 11 LeManna/Shutterstock.com; p. 13 alexkich/Shutterstock.com; p. 15 michaeljung/Shutterstock.com; p. 17 Serhii Bobyk/Shutterstock.com; p. 19 The Num Phanu Studio/Shutterstock.com; p. 21 vystekimages/Shutterstock.com; p. 22 brittak/E+/Getty Images.

Cataloging-in-Publication Data

Names: Honders, Christine.
Title: Mechanics / Christine Honders.
Description: New York : PowerKids Press, 2020. | Series: Helpers in our community | Includes glossary and index.
Identifiers: ISBN 9781725308268 (pbk.) | ISBN 9781725308282 (library bound) | ISBN 9781725308275 (6 pack)
Subjects: LCSH: Mechanics–Juvenile literature.
Classification: LCC TL147.H66 2020 | DDC 629.04-dc23
Manufactured in the United States of America

CPSIA Compliance Information: Batch #CWPK20. For Further Information contact Rosen Publishing, New York, New York at 1-800-237-9932.

CONTENTS

Under the Hood 4
Mechanics Know Machines . . 6
Simple Machines 8
Compound Machines 10
Motors 12
When the Car Breaks Down . . 14
Power Tools 16
Car Doctors 18
Ready for Anything 20
Mechanics Move the World! . 22
Glossary 23
Index 24
Websites 24

Under the Hood

Have you ever looked under the hood of a car? There are a lot of parts in there! They work together to make the car move. Most people don't really know how this works. But **mechanics** do!

Mechanics Know Machines

Machines make our lives better every day. Mechanics know how machines work. They know what each part does and how they fit together. They use special tools to figure out what's wrong with a car. They can take machines apart, fix them, and put them back together.

Simple Machines

Simple machines are tools that make work easier. Ramps make it easier to move heavy things. Levers make the force a person can create greater. Wheels help us move things more easily and quickly. These are all simple machines.

9

Compound Machines

Compound machines are made up of two or more simple machines. Think of a bicycle. You can see wheels, axles, and levers at work in a bicycle. Cars and trucks are compound machines made up of hundreds of simple machines! Mechanics understand all these parts and how they work.

Motors

Motors are compound machines. Motors turn other kinds of **energy** into **mechanical** energy. In a car motor, this energy makes the car run. Many mechanics work on motors in cars, trucks, and boats. Some mechanics fix smaller motors for smaller machines, such as lawn mowers.

When the Car Breaks Down

Imagine your family is ready to go on a trip, but the car won't start. Call the mechanic! They'll help you get the car to their shop even if it's not running. They'll figure out and fix what's wrong. Then you can go have fun!

Power Tools

Most people don't have the right tools to fix cars. Mechanics use special power tools. These tools help them tighten **screws** stronger and faster than any person can. Huge lifts raise cars into the air. Mechanics can easily check for problems under the car.

Car Doctors

Mechanics are car doctors. They don't just fix cars. They tell the owner what went wrong. They sometimes show the owner how to take care of the car. Mechanics also give cars a yearly checkup. They test the brakes and tires for safety.

Ready for Anything

Cars can break down at any time. Mechanics have to be ready day or night. They work long hours and often work on weekends. They're in the shop during hot summers and cold winters. Mechanics work very hard to get us where we need to go.

Mechanics Move the World!

Mechanics keep our cars, trucks, and buses running so we can go to school or work. They fix the trucks and machines that help build our homes. They fix boats that bring food and goods we need to our communities.

Mechanics move the world, one motor at a time!

GLOSSARY

compound: Made up of two or more parts.

energy: The power to work or act.

mechanic: A person who fixes machines.

mechanical: Having to do with machines.

motor: A machine that makes motion or power for doing work.

screw: A small, often metal object that's used to hold things together.

INDEX

B
boats, 12, 22
buses, 22

C
cars, 4, 6, 10, 12, 14, 16, 18, 20, 22
compound machines, 10, 12

L
levers, 8, 10

M
machines, 6, 8, 10, 12, 22

motors, 12, 22

R
ramps, 8

S
simple machines, 8, 20

T
tools, 6, 8, 16
trucks, 10, 12, 22

W
wheels, 8, 10

WEBSITES

Due to the changing nature of Internet links, PowerKids Press has developed an online list of websites related to the subject of this book. This site is updated regularly. Please use this link to access the list: www.powerkidslinks.com/HIOC/mechanics